The Heart of A Wounded Hero:
Above and Beyond
By Michelle Rider

This is a work of fiction. Similarities to real people, places, or events are entirely coincidental.

ABOVE AND BEYOND: HEART OF A WOUNDED HERO

First edition. March 8, 2023.

Copyright © 2023 Michelle Rider.

ISBN: 979-8215728147

Written by Michelle Rider.

Table of Contents

For all of those who have fought or are fighting for our freedom.

We owe you everything.

Thank you for your service.

Prologue

"**H**art! Get back! It's too late!" my commanding officer, Zeb, screams at me.

"No! I won't leave him! I can't!" I say, rushing toward the burning Humvee.

I can hear him whining, can feel the terror racing through him in his whimpers. Each howl, each cry tears through me like a knife.

"Ember!" Zeb says again. Everything in me tells me to listen to my commanding officer, but the thought of Romeo hurting fuels my movements.

As I reach the door to the Humvee, an explosion blows the window in front of me, and I throw my hands up to protect my face. I can feel the heat from the flames and glass shards cutting through my skin, but I don't stop. I can't. Romeo lets out a scream that stops my heart. There is now fire roaring through the open window, the sound almost deafening. The only thing louder is the now agonizing yelping coming from Romeo who is stuck behind a giant wall of flames.

"No!" I scream as I grab the door handle, ignoring the searing pain that shoots up my arms as the fire licks at my skin.

"Romeo!"

I feel arms pulling at me from behind as I scream and put everything I have into getting to my best friend, my partner.

Time stands still as I fight against the people pulling at me and against the fire raging in front of me. Forward, backward, either way, leads to pain. Romeo's howls die off as another explosion rocks the vehicle, sending me and everyone behind me flying backward through the air. I land in a heap on the ground, twenty feet from the burning Humvee, the heat of the flames still burning my skin.

People surround me in a rush in an attempt to tend to what is left of the skin on my forearms and hands. But I don't care.

"*Romeo! Romeo!*" I scream as the tears flow freely down my face. I don't even feel the pain in my arms because the devastation in my heart is so much worse.

"He's gone, Hart. There's nothing we can do," Zeb says from right next to me. I can feel him holding me down, pressing firmly on my shoulders to keep me on the ground.

One final explosion rocks the Humvee sending debris and ash reigning down on us Zeb covers my head with his body to protect me, but it doesn't matter. Nothing matters anymore. I failed him. I failed Romeo and he paid the ultimate price.

I will never forgive myself.

I shoot up in bed with a gasp, my hand instinctively grasping my chest where the pain is the worst. I clutch at the tank top I am wearing as if that will relieve the pain. But it won't. Nothing ever will.

Almost a year has passed, and I can't shake these nightmares. It is the same thing every night. I watch him die. I watch my beloved partner and best friend, Romeo, die. I trained him from a pup and spent all eight years of his life with him. And in the blink of an eye, he was gone, taken from me. I watched him torturously suffer and burn to death and there was nothing I could do about it. I tried, but I failed.

Rubbing my eyes, I glance at the clock on my bedside table and see it is just past six in the morning. I know I won't be getting any more sleep, so I get up and prepare for my day. Not that I have anything to do. Just therapy.

My shoulders slump at the thought. The last thing I want to do is sit and talk about what happened… again. But it is required – part of my recovery. If only they knew. There is no recovering from this.

I get up and decide to go for a run before I have to get ready for my appointment. As always, I pull on my long-sleeved Army shirt to cover my arms. I went through so many surgeries and skin grafts to get to where I am now. The skin is still so sensitive, and it looks awful. I am not saying anything against the doctors who worked on me; I know they did their best with what they had to work with. But I learned early on that I earn too many stares and whispers if I don't keep them covered. I even wear gloves to cover my hands. I know I am lucky that I regained use of them after everything. It was touch and go for a while and there is so much physical and physiotherapy that I still have to do on a daily basis. But the aches and pains are constant. The only thing is, I don't know if the pain is real, or if it is my way of torturing myself for what I let happen.

I do what I always do when I run and push myself to the point where my mind is focused only on my next step. I have found that the faster I run, the harder I work, the less my mind wanders into dangerous territory. Each step is my own form of therapy because it is the only time when I am not thinking of him or the time I failed him.

Ten miles and an hour later and I am beyond exhausted, but it worked. I haven't thought of anything since I left my house. I am dripping with sweat, my shirt drenched to the point where it is sticking to me everywhere. It is at times like this that I miss my days in the service. There was a strict schedule, someone making sure my every move was planned. Now, there is just me and the thoughts that will never go away.

I spend a long time in the shower. I have massages and stretching that I do under the water because, for some reason, it doesn't hurt as much in here. My fingers rub along the raised, puckered skin, trying to increase the blood flow and relieve some of the pressure that I feel each and every minute of each and every day. There are still parts of my hands where I don't have any feeling, but they keep assuring me that I will get there.

By the time the water runs cold, I know I need to get moving if I am going to make it to my appointment on time. I have to see Dr. Williamson, or Antonia, twice a week as part of my healing process. I was honorably discharged after the event, but they don't just send you on your merry way, especially if you were injured. The Army makes sure they keep up with your progress. They monitor everything, including my mental status.

Antonia is waiting for me in her office when I get there. She has the same annoying, pleasant smile on her face as I take my seat across from her. I really do like her, and she has helped me a lot over the past six months, but I just don't see the point of this anymore. There is nothing they will ever be able to do for me to make this all go away. The memories are permanently etched in my brain.

"Ember, how are you doing today?" Antonia asks in her overly chipper voice. I have to fight the extreme urge to roll my eyes.

"I'm good. Same as always," I say, trying to sound better than I actually feel.

"That's great, Ember," she says. She looks extra happy today, and for some reason, that puts me on edge. Something is up and I don't like it one bit.

"I made some calls since the last time you were here, and I think I have an idea that will really put you on the right path," she says with an eager smile.

"Okaaaaay," I say, not liking where this is going. Usually, when she has an idea, I end up doing some weird activity that makes me very uncomfortable and doesn't help at all.

"There is a man on the other side of town who trains dogs for injured veterans," she starts, but I cut her off.

"No."

"Ember," she says, but I hold my hand up to stop her.

"I can't, Antonia. I'm sorry, I really am. But I just... can't."

She gets up from her desk and comes around to take the open chair next to me. She places her hand on my forearm. I have a hoodie and my gloves on to hide my injuries, but she always goes out of her way to try and show me that they aren't a big deal.

"Ember, please. Hear me out. I can't even imagine what you went through. You have been to hell and back. But it is time for you to do something for yourself. I think it would be... beneficial for you to work with dogs again. I don't expect you to run out and adopt ten puppies or start working as a dog trainer again. I just want you to be around them, and get reacquainted with the idea. I want you to prove to yourself that you can do this," she says. She has that sympathetic, sorrow-filled gaze in her eyes, and I hate it because it makes me want to run.

"Antonia," I say in a whiney voice that I despise. "I... don't think I can."

I suddenly can't sit still. The thought of being around dogs again makes me want to puke. After Romeo, after watching him burn to death, I don't know *how* to be around them. I have gone out of my way to avoid dogs, even going as far as crossing the street to avoid walking near one.

"Ember. You can do this. Just go. Once. Give it a shot. If you come back next time and tell me you couldn't do it, then fine. We will figure something else out. But you have to try. At least once," she says, patting my arm before she gets up and grabs a piece of paper off her desk.

She hands it to me. When I reach for it, I see that my hands are shaking, so much so that I have a hard time reading what is written on the paper.

Colby Masterson. Alpha Dog Training. 1010 Pine Street.

I slide the piece of paper into my pocket, not sure how I am going to do this. So many thoughts are racing through my mind. Memories of meeting Romeo for the first time, lying in bed with his head on my chest, each training session, each lick and kiss... it is all too much. I feel a few tears fall and swipe at them angrily with my gloved fingers.

Unfortunately for me, Antonia knows exactly what to say to get me off my ass. "Romeo would want you to be happy, Ember."

Well, shit.

"**G**reat job today, everyone! Again, I can't thank you enough for your help with this project. We will see you next week," I say to the ten men and women standing in front of me with the puppies they are training for my program.

Alpha Dog Training is my baby, and I pour so much of myself into everything that we do here. As an injured vet myself, I know the importance of the healing process and I make sure that each and every dog that we train is well prepared to help the vet that they are assigned to.

"When is the injured vet coming?" Dave, my business partner, asks me. He and I served in the same unit in the Army and when we were both injured and discharged, we decided we wanted to do everything we could to give back to our brothers and sisters who need us.

I check my watch. "In about fifteen minutes," I say as I make my way around the floor, cleaning up from the last class.

"What's her story? Do you know?" Dave asks.

I shrug. "Not really sure. I know she trained dogs for the Army and was discharged about a year ago. Her therapist didn't want to say much else. She told me it was her story to tell, and I respect that."

"Do you want me to stick around?" he asks.

"Nah. I would like to meet her and get a feel for where she is. I don't want to overwhelm her with too much," I say.

"Call me if you need anything," he says as he heads out.

I spend some time straightening up the training floor and reorganizing the chairs. My time in the Army and the things they drilled into my very being stay with me. I need everything to be organized and in its rightful place or it drives me crazy. By the time I make it back to my office, I notice that the vet should have been here ten minutes ago. I debate whether I should call her therapist but decide against it and give her a little bit longer. She might just be running late.

"Tonka! Let's go for a quick walk, bud," I say, calling my Golden Retriever to my side.

I laugh when he comes trotting into the office carrying his stuffed cat toy, something he doesn't go anywhere without.

"You got your kitty, bud? You bringing him with us?" I ask. I have a terrible habit of speaking to Tonka as if he will answer me, and he does, in his own way.

He takes off out of the office and toward the front door and I follow closely behind. When we make it outside, I notice a car parked at the end of the lot. It isn't one I have never seen here before. Tonka and I head in that direction, and I see someone sitting on the bench on the other side of the car. Whoever it is has their head in their hands, and they are leaning forward with their elbows on their knees. They are rocking back and forth, their body in constant motion. I see a long, dirty blonde ponytail hanging off to the side, so I am pretty sure it is a woman. Her entire body seems to be shaking as she bounces her legs up and down. I can feel the anxiety pouring off her and it causes a chill to run down my spine.

Tonka, who has no understanding whatsoever of personal space, runs right up to her and shoves his kitty in between her knees and in her face. She startles, jumping back and cringing away from him as if she is afraid.

"Tonka! Back off," I command, and he takes a step away and sits, still wagging his tail excitedly at his new friend.

I jog over but stop short when I get my first good look at her. She is beyond gorgeous with her long blonde hair and bright green eyes the color of the trees. She has a tiny, slightly upturned nose and high cheekbones and I have to force myself to close my mouth so that I don't drool. But it is the overwhelming fear in her eyes that tears right through me.

"Hi. Sorry about this knucklehead," I say as I rub Tonka behind the ears. "He loves people and has a hard time understanding that not everyone loves dogs. He won't hurt you, though. He might lick you to death, but other than that, you have nothing to worry about."

She scoots as far away from him as possible. I can see how fast she is breathing; her hand is clutching her chest as if she might pass out.

"Hey. It's okay. You don't have to be afraid," I say, taking a tentative step toward her.

She turns away from us, gasping for breath, whispering things to herself. I can't quite make out the words, but I do hear "Romeo" several times.

I decide a different tactic might work. "Tonka, go back inside," I say, to which he takes off to the front door of my office. I watch him until he lies down at the front door. I know he won't move until I release him.

I hesitantly take the seat next to her, far enough away that I am not touching her. I am seriously fighting the urge to wrap her in my arms, to tell her everything will be okay, to hold her and take all her fears away. But I have seen this before in many of the vets that we work with. Something from her past is haunting her. That doesn't stop me from wanting to ease her pain.

I see that she is wearing gloves and I have a feeling that has a lot to do with whatever this is.

"I'm Colby. Colby Masterson. I own this place. Are you Ember?" I ask, trying to keep my voice soft and calm. Just being this close to her has my heart racing for some reason. I am not the type of guy that gets hung up on a pretty face, but there is more to this woman, and everything in me wants to figure it out. I have this overwhelming need to protect her, to ease her pain.

She nods once. She has relaxed a bit since I sent Tonka away but is still tense. I can see the tightness in her shoulders, and the strain in her muscles as she wraps her arms around herself.

"Are you afraid of dogs, Ember?"

She shakes her head no rapidly.

"What can I do?" I ask, desperate to help her, to calm her down.

"Nothing," she says, so quietly I almost miss it.

"There has to be something I can do," I say, taking a chance and sliding toward her slightly.

She watches my movement but doesn't say anything.

She shakes her head again. "There's nothing anybody can do. I shouldn't have come here. This was a mistake," she says as she jumps to her feet.

I can't let her leave like this. I can't let her leave at all. Something in her calls to me and I need to figure out what it is. I instinctively reach out and take her hand.

Her movements stop as she turns to stare at my hand holding hers, but I don't let go. I can't.

She looks confused like she doesn't understand the touch. I get the feeling that she wears these gloves as a shield, to protect herself from something.

"Please," I say, softer this time, patting the bench next to me.

She hesitantly slides back down to the bench. She tries to pull her hand from mine, but I don't let her. I have a feeling she needs the contact, almost as much as I do right now. I don't know what it is, but her fear, her anxiousness hurts me, and I have this immense need to ease it.

"Why do you care?" she asks. It is not a cynical question like she doesn't understand how anyone would want to help. It is more out of curiosity. Her tone is soft and gentle, her voice melodious.

"I'm a vet, too. I don't like seeing you... uh, people upset," I say.

Smooth, Colby. Real smooth.

"What all did Antonia tell you about me?" she asks.

"Nothing, really. Just that you would be coming in to check out the place. She seemed to think it would help you in some way," I say. As the words come out, I notice her relax a little, as if my not knowing her circumstance is a good thing.

"She was wrong. Nothing here will help," she says.

"Why?" I ask. A simple question, but for people like us, who carry so much with us, it can mean so much more.

She pulls her hand again, and this time I release her. If she is going to talk to me, she needs to know that she can trust me. If not touching me makes her more comfortable, then that's fine. But I don't let her go far as I scoot a tad closer to her. Her eyes shift at my movement, but she doesn't move away. I'll take that as a little victory.

"I don't want to talk about it," she says.

"Do you want to take a walk? We don't have to talk. I just think it may make you more comfortable with me," I say, motioning toward the park across the street.

She glances at the park and then back to me. There is curiosity in her gaze. I can tell she wants to, but her mind is fighting her.

When she eventually nods, I want to pump my fist in the air, but I don't.

"Do you mind if Tonka comes with us?"

"Do you mind if Tonka comes with us?" Colby asks.

I don't know what it is about this man, but he oozes comfort and strength. His smile is soothing, and it makes me want to curl up in his arms and pour out my soul. I don't understand it at all, but for some reason, I want to be around him.

I shock myself when I nod at him. Why am I even doing this? What good could possibly come from any of this? A walk with a complete stranger. Spending time with him and his dog.

At my nod, he whistles, and Tonka comes trotting over to us, his stuffed kitty in his mouth. I don't know how he manages, but his giant tongue is hanging out around the side of the toy. I find myself smiling, but quickly wipe it away when he catches me and smirks.

"Come on," he says as he places his palm on the small of my back. The simple gesture sends a chill through me. If I could, I am sure that my skin would have broken out in goosebumps at the contact.

We cross the street and enter the park. Tonka takes off to chase a squirrel, stuffed kitty, and all. I wonder what he thinks he would do if it caught it. It's not like he could fit it and his toy in his mouth at the same time.

"You do like dogs," Colby says with a grin.

"I used to," I say simply, not wanting to go into my fucked-up history.

"What changed?" he asks.

"You said we didn't have to talk," I say in a grumble. I hate that I am being so bitchy with him, but it is a defense mechanism that I can't shake.

"You're right. I did say that. So, I'll talk. I'll tell you all about me so that you have no choice but to realize how amazing I am and how you know you can trust me with your deepest darkest secrets," he says with an adorable smirk as he winks at me.

His gaze is constantly shifting between me and Tonka. It's almost like he can't decide who he needs to watch closer.

"You're cocky," I say, nudging him with my shoulder.

"No. Confident. There's a huge difference," he says.

He whistles for Tonka, who immediately stops what he is doing and trots over to Colby's side.

"He is very well trained," I say. Romeo would do the same thing… if he still could.

"Well, I am the best at what I do," he says. "And that is cocky."

He nudges me back. I like this playful side to him. It makes him seem more real.

I laugh a little.

"There it is. I knew I could get you to smile," he says as he grabs a stick and tosses it to Tonka.

"Cocky," I say again with a small smile. "Alright. Tell me all about the amazing Colby Masterson."

"Well, I served for eight years before I was honorably discharged. Got injured on a mission and couldn't continue. My business partner, Dave, and I were in the same unit. When we both got injured and sent home, we decided we wanted to do what we could to help other injured vets. So, we started Alpha Dog Training. Tonka is my best friend. He's been with me since I got home. We live a few miles away on the river. I am a terrible cook, but I love to eat. My favorite thing to do is read. I like long walks in the park and candlelight dinners by the fire," he says, but at the word, my face drops.

Fire.

It's everywhere.

I can feel the heat on my skin. I can hear Romeo's cries.

My vision starts to fade, and I stumble to a bench a few feet away, barely making it before I collapse there. My entire body is trembling and am quickly spiraling out of control.

"Ember. Talk to me, honey. What's going on?" Colby says from right next to me. Before I can protest, he has his arms wrapped around me and my head on his chest. I don't know why, but it calms me slightly.

I try to focus on my breathing, just like Antonia taught me when I have one of these panic attacks.

In.

Out.

In.

Out.

"That's it. Nice and slow. Focus on the air moving through your lungs. Feel it move in and out of you. Let it carry the pain with it," he says, and I blanch. Those are the exact words that Antonia uses with me.

"How?" I manage to say between breaths.

He is still holding me close, his one hand on my head, holding it to his chest, the other running up and down my arm. I worry that he may feel my raised skin, the abnormal hideousness of my body. But if he does, it doesn't deter him from trying to calm me.

"I've been there, Em. I may not know what you went through, but I know how to help. Antonia helped me when I got back and couldn't shake the nightmares," he says.

He was a patient of Antonia's? He needed her help when he got back. That means he must have been through something awful, too.

I am a terrible person. I have been living as if I am the only one who knows pain. I have been isolating myself because I felt I deserved it. But there are other people, other vets, who have been through things just like me, maybe even worse.

That thought sobers me and I pull back from his hold. He reluctantly lets me go, and his hands slide slowly down my arms until he is holding my hands in his.

"Thank you," I say.

"Hey. It's no big deal. We have to do what we can for each other, right? If my experiences can help you, then it was worth it," he says as he reaches up and cups my cheek.

I close my eyes and lean into his touch, needing the contact right now. I didn't realize how much I needed this until this very moment.

Before I know what is happening, the words are tumbling from my mouth.

"My dog's name was Romeo. I spent my time in the service training service dogs," I whisper, not sure why I am telling him this.

Colby drops his hand and wraps his arm around my shoulder. "Tell me."

"We were on a mission in Afghanistan. It was supposed to be in and out, we weren't supposed to see any action. Just clear the road and go back," I say. My heart is pounding in my chest as I think about it and say the words out loud for the first time in months.

"Hart. Take Romeo and report back in fifteen," Zeb says.

"Come on, boy. Time to work," I say as Romeo, and I hop out of the Humvee.

"Em, it's ok. That's enough for today," Colby says, bringing me back before I disappear too far down the rabbit hole.

"What? You don't want to know the rest?" I ask, confused. That's not normally the way this works.

"I do, but when you are ready. I don't want to cause you pain by making you relive it. We can do it a bit at a time. I'm in no rush," he says.

I feel something on my leg and look down to see Tonka is resting his chin on my thigh. His stuffed kitty is on the ground next to him.

"She's okay, buddy," Colby says as he ruffles the hair on Tonka's head.

"I'm sorry," I say as I push away from him and stand. I feel so vulnerable right now. I can't believe I was telling someone I barely know what happened.

"Hey. It's just you and me here. Well, and Tonka, but I'm pretty sure he won't tell anyone. You're safe with me, I promise," Colby says, and I think I believe him.

"Come on. Why don't you let me take you to get some lunch? I know a great burger place," Colby says as he stands.

He holds his hand out to me, palm up, and waits patiently for me to decide what to do.

My mind is still recovering from the little bit of my past that I just relived. I know I am not there anymore, but for some reason, just hearing that word put me right back there. It's been a trigger for me since the accident. No matter where I am, no matter what I am doing, that word sends me on a downward spiral like a raging tornado, ready to tear me apart.

I stare into Colby's eyes, the gentleness and strength that they exude make me want to disappear there. I felt safe for the first time in a year when he was holding me, and that scares the ever-living shit out of me. It made me want to curl up in his lap and let him hold me forever.

Tonka lets out a small whine, almost daring me to take Colby's outstretched hand, so I do. This might be a big mistake, opening myself up to someone, but for some reason, Colby seems worth the risk.

The moment her hand slides into mine is the moment I know that this woman is my future. I hate that she is going through so much. I hate that she lives with this pain. I know how it can haunt you. I've been there. Shit, it took me years to get over the nightmares. I still have them every once in a while, but they have become few and far between at this point.

What I feel with Ember is more than I have ever felt with another person before. I hold onto her gloved hand as we walk back to my office, not willing to let her go. I can't wait until she feels comfortable enough with me to let me really touch her, to feel her skin. Whatever she is hiding won't matter. I have a feeling I know what it is – probably the same thing I hid for a long time. But I will let her come to me in her time. I just won't give up.

"Do you want to ride with me? It's not that far," I say. "Let me just drop Tonka off in my office and we can go."

"Uh, sure. That's fine," she says.

I release her hand and unlock the door. Just as I am about to call Tonka over, I see Ember tentatively reach her hand out to him, running her fingers briefly through the hair on his head. She ends by tugging slightly on his ears, something that Tonka loves more than anything.

I don't say anything because, for some reason, I feel like this is a big deal for her. I know that whatever happened to her, involved her dog, Romeo. She got that far in her story. But when I saw her slipping away, I decided to end it, not wanting her to be in pain. I meant what I said to her - she will tell me, but in her time.

I smile when she looks up and catches me watching her.

"Sorry," she says as she pulls her hand away. Tonka doesn't like the loss of her touch and he grabs onto her hand with his mouth gently. The movement catches her off guard and she yanks her hand away so quickly that Tonka is left standing there with her glove in his mouth.

She gasps and quickly tries to cover her hand. I don't let her hide from me though. I step up to her and take her hand, pulling against her hold as she tries to cover it with her sleeve.

"Don't. Don't hide from me," I say softly as I pull her hand out and place a kiss right in the center of her palm.

"Colby," she says, and my heart breaks at the desperation that I hear there.

I turn her hand over and place kisses on each finger, on the scarred skin of the back of her hand, on her wrist, and then back on her palm. I can hear her harsh breathing as I continue to prove to her that her scars don't bother me. I have my own that she will soon see.

I reach out and take her other hand, pulling that glove off as well. She fights me, but not too hard, so I know she needs this right now. I repeat the same actions on that hand, kissing all over her damaged skin. She shudders slightly and lets out the most adorable sigh. I can feel her relaxing with each kiss, with each touch, and I love that.

"You are beautiful, Em. Every single inch of you. We all have scars, some physical, some emotional. It is what you do with them, and how you overcome them that matters most," I say as I take her hand, and slide it under my shirt so that she can feel the same skin on my sides and chest.

She gasps at my revelation.

"Colby, I'm so sorry," she says as she runs her fingers over the marred skin on my body.

I want to reply, but I am too busy enjoying the feel of her fingers running over my body. I close my eyes and just take it in. Her closeness, her floral scent, her touch. I know we just met today, but this moment right here is bigger than anything I have ever experienced. It is two people sharing something, a simple touch that proves they are not alone.

"What happened?" she asks as she pulls her hands away and lowers my shirt.

"IED. Caught us by surprise. Dave and I were traveling back to the base after a mission. The blast sent us flying. I got out right away, but he was stuck inside. I couldn't leave him, so I fought through the flames to pull him out. He took the brunt of it; he suffered third-degree burns on his legs. I had the most damage on my torso. It took months to be able to function normally. But I fought my way back. So did he. That's why we do what we do. We know what it's like to want to give up."

She is quiet for a minute, fidgeting back and forth. I don't miss that she slid her hands into the pocket of her hoodie. She is hiding them again, but I don't mind because she let me see her, even if it was for a few seconds.

"Thank you for sharing that with me," she says quietly.

I can tell that she is getting overwhelmed with everything, so I turn and open the door, following Tonka in to get him set up in my office while we go grab lunch.

When I come back out, she is waiting for me, standing there with her gloves back on.

I can't help it; I walk right up to her and pull her into my arms. She comes willingly and wraps hers around my waist, leaning her head on my chest.

"I'm sorry for what you went through," she says into my chest.

"You're not alone, Em. I'm here now and I'm going to help you through this. We'll get through it together," I say as I place a kiss on the top of her head.

"Why do I feel so safe with you?" she asks, but I don't think she meant to say it out loud.

"Because. You are. I won't let anything happen to you, Em. I promise. I don't know what this is, what is happening, but I swear to you that I want it with everything in me," I say, pulling her back so that I can look into her deep green eyes.

A blush covers her cheeks, and I reach up to run my fingers along them.

I lean forward and place a kiss on her forehead, lingering there for a few seconds.

She takes a deep breath and lets it out slowly, leaning into me. She squeezes me once before she steps back and smiles.

"You said something about burgers?" she asks.

I smile and pull her to my side.

"I sure did."

I don't know what the future holds, but for the first time in a really long time, I am excited to find out.

Coby wasn't kidding when he said he likes to eat. He put away two cheeseburgers to my one and more French fries than I have ever seen one person eat in one sitting. I could barely finish mine, so he did.

"You are a beast," I say with a smile, laughing as he polishes off every last bit of food on our plates.

"Told you. I love to eat," he says as he leans back and pats his still flat stomach. I know he keeps himself in shape. I felt the hardness of his body when he placed my hands there earlier. It took everything in me not to drool as I felt the ridges of each muscle. I didn't even notice the scars at first, and I know that was his point.

We talked all through lunch about everything and anything. Our families, our time in the service (except for the incident), and our hobbies. It turns out we have a lot in common. We both love to run. We both miss the regimented schedules of our time in the service. We both love dogs. I did tell him a little more about Romeo, about how I trained him and our life together. It felt really good to talk about him. I may have pictures of him all over my house, but I have spent the past year avoiding them, afraid to really look at them and remember what it was like with him by my side. He really was the most amazing dog. He wasn't just a pet or a partner. He was my best friend, the only one I could say anything to and not be judged. Even now, after everything that happened, I know he wouldn't blame me. He had the purest soul, the gentlest heart. He was faithful and everything anyone could ever want in a friend.

"Where did you just go?" Colby asks as he reaches out to take my hand. "You lost your smile."

"Just thinking about Romeo and how much I miss him," I say.

"He sounds amazing from what you've told me," Colby says.

A tear slips free, and I can feel myself spiraling again as my pulse increases. I am suddenly finding it very hard to breathe.

I stand abruptly and almost knock over my chair. "I should go."

"Don't run, Ember. Let me help," Colby says as he comes around to fix my chair.

"I can't. I can't do this. I'm sorry," I say as I back away from him.

"Em, please," he says, and I hate the pain I see in his eyes.

"I'm sorry," I say one more time before I turn and run from the restaurant. The problem is, I came with Colby, so I don't have a car.

It doesn't matter. I take off at a sprint, pushing myself harder and harder so that my mind clears, and I forget the pain of everything. I hate myself right now. I am a coward. Colby was offering me everything I have ever wanted – someone to give me strength, to help me bear the weight on my shoulders. But I can't handle that right now. He made me feel again, and that's something I didn't want. When you open yourself up to someone, you invite the pain of them leaving you. Whether it is intentional or not, they always leave.

I don't really know where I am going, I just run until my legs are ready to give out and I collapse onto a bench.

I realize that I ran right to the bench that Colby and I were sitting in not too long ago. I don't have the energy to even contemplate the meaning behind that, so I just get up and make my way back toward his office where my car is parked.

Just as I am about to exit the park, I see Colby drive up. He gets out of his car and just stands there, his hands linked behind the back of his head.

I quickly duck behind a tree to stay out of sight.

"Stupid, stupid, stupid," he says to the sky as he begins pacing back and forth. "I pushed her too hard."

He slams his car door and head inside. He is only gone for a second before he reappears with Tonka at his side.

"I know, bud. I fucked up. But I'll fix it, I promise," he says as he lets him in and climbs in behind him.

I watch him drive away.

I know I need to talk to him. But I just can't right now. He brought out emotions in me today that I thought were dead. When I woke up in the hospital after one of my surgeries, I realized that the only way to avoid pain is to not let anyone close, animals or people. Yet in a matter of a few hours, this man and his amazing dog tunneled right into my heart, and I don't know how to handle that.

I wait until he is gone from sight before I make my way over to my car and drive home. I don't know where to go from here. Do I take the chance and let him in? Do I risk everything, including my heart, and open myself up to the potential hurt?

I wish I knew the answer to those questions. Well, them and all the other five million questions running through my head right now. I don't want to feel.

No, that's not it. I don't want to hurt. I don't want this pain anymore. But I don't know what to do about it.

I have spent the past few hours driving around aimlessly, searching for Ember. Her car was at my office when I picked mine up, but when I drove by later, it was gone. She is running. That much I'm sure of. I just wish I knew what she was running from.

By the time I make it back to my apartment, it is dark. I feel hopeless, hollow from these feelings racing through me. How can someone I have known for less than a day create such intense emotions? It makes no sense. All I know is that when I am with her, I feel complete like I finally found what has been missing from my life. I can still feel her in my arms, can still smell her strawberry shampoo. I thought I was taking things slow enough, allowing her to just get to know me, but I must have done something to scare her off.

I remember how lost I felt when I first came home. After the trauma of my injuries and then enduring the countless surgeries to try and put me back together, I felt useless. I went from being needed, to being nothing. I think a lot of injured vets go through that, at least, that's the main thing I hear in our group therapy sessions at the VA. Yeah, I still go to those, years later, because they help. I only go about once every few months when I feel myself slipping. But sometimes it is just nice to hear that others are feeling the same way. That I am not alone.

It took me years to get to where I am today. I know Ember has only been home for about one year, and I could tell today that she is still struggling with everything.

I can't just sit here and wait. I grab my phone and call Antonia, hoping she will give me something on her.

"Hello?" she answers on the second ring.

"Antonia, hi. It's Colby Masterson," I say.

"Colby. How are you? How did things go today with Ember?" she asks.

I sigh. "They were going well for a while, but I think I spooked her," I say as I pace back and forth in my living room.

Tonka is watching me closely. I know he can feel the tension rolling off me.

"What happened?" she asks.

I tell her about how we met. I tell her about the connection I felt with her and how we went for lunch together. Every detail up to the point where she ran.

"You have to give me something, Antonia. I need to find her. I need to be there for her," I say sounding desperate, which is exactly how I feel.

"You feel something for her," she says. It's not a question. She can hear it in my voice.

"I do. She's special, and I know she needs me, just like I need her."

"She's fighting some pretty big demons, Colby," she says. "You have to be prepared to deal with that. I fear it may trigger some things from your past."

I think about that for a minute. Is that something I am willing to risk for Ember?

Hell yes.

"I don't care, Antonia. I can't explain it, but I know that she needs me. Not just somebody, me. Shit, I'm not making any sense," I say in a grumble, running my hand through my hair roughly, pulling at the ends.

"Tell me why Colby. Why do feel so connected to her of all people?" she asks as she slips into therapist mode. I haven't been to her office as a patient for a few years now having graduated to the group sessions. But she knows exactly what to say to make me feel like I am sitting in front of her again, pouring out my soul.

"I... can't really explain it. When I saw her for the first time, sure, I thought she was beautiful. But when I saw her hands, felt the pain that she went through," I say, but Antonia cuts me off.

"Wait. She showed you her hands?"

"Well, not intentionally. Tonka pulled one of her gloves off. I wouldn't let her put it back on because I could see exactly what she was trying to hide and I wanted her to know that with or without the scars, she is the most breathtaking woman I have ever seen," I say. I feel like I am a rambling teenager, unable to express my feelings.

"She lives in the Woodbridge Ave apartment complex. Apartment 3A," she says quickly.

I pause for a moment, wondering why she is so willing to give up the information so freely.

"Don't let her hide from you, Colby," she says as I contemplate everything.

"Why are you suddenly so willing to give me information?" I ask.

"She has been hiding behind those gloves and long-sleeved shirts since I have known her. She has never, ever, willingly shown anyone her skin. The fact that she let you see them, hell, touch them, means something big, Colby. Don't let her hide. Please. She needs you," she says.

I am stunned to the point where I slide down the wall that I was leaning on until my butt slams into the floor. I don't know whether to smile or cry for this woman who has hidden her beauty from the world for so long.

"I won't, Antonia. I need her, too."

"I know you do. That's why I sent her to you. You need each other," she says, and then ends the call.

Tonka comes over to me and lays his head on my lap. I absently stroke his head as I go over everything that happened today. I knew the moment I saw her, before I even saw her face, that she was something special. I couldn't put my finger on it – it was just a feeling, a sixth sense almost, that told me there was something there. Something important, hell, life changing.

Then, when I looked into her eyes, that feeling became a tidal wave of emotion, knocking me on my ass from its intensity. I felt like the air was sucked from my lungs. I have never felt something like that before.

I am moving before I realize it as I grab my keys and open the front door. Tonka whines behind me, stopping me in my tracks.

"I have to do this, buddy. I have to find her and let her know I'm with her, no matter what," I say to him.

He gives me a look that tells me he understands. I swear he nods, too, but I shake my head. Maybe I'm just going crazy.

If I am, I'll be damned sure I enjoy the ride.

You'd better be ready, Em. I'm coming for you.

I let the hot water rush over my body. I have already done my exercises and stretches. Now, I am just imagining the water washing away my pain, my fear, my worry that I have fucked up.

I have spent the past few hours berating myself for how I ran away from Colby. Literally. Ran. Like a damned coward. I'm sure he wants nothing to do with me now. The crazy woman who can't let the past go. Who lets it haunt her, every second, of every day. I can't even hear the word fi... nope. Not going there. Not after everything today brought me.

I tuck my chin to my chest, letting the water flow over my neck and head. My legs feel weak from the strenuous work I put them through today. Not only my morning run but running from Colby.

I turn off the water, ready to just crawl under the covers and end the day. Just as I am drying off my hair, there is a loud banging at my door.

I ignore it at first, thinking that maybe someone just has the wrong door, but it continues.

Who the hell is banging on my door at ten o'clock?

I slip on my robe, ready to just go tell them to fuck off so I can wallow in self-pity and enjoy my misery.

I am just tying my robe shut as I yank open the front door.

The words die in my throat as I see a very disheveled Colby standing there. His eyes are wild, his hair is sticking up in all directions, and even his clothes look worn and wrinkled.

"Colby? What are you doing here?" I ask as I try to pull my robe tighter around me. It is then that I realize my biggest mistake. My forearms and hands are on full display. I try to slam the door in his face when he takes a few steps toward me until he is right on top of me. I have to tilt my head back to look at him.

"Colby?" I ask again, but the words are barely audible.

He raises his hands and places them on my cheeks, tilting my head back even further.

"You ran," he says softly as he stares into my eyes.

I try to turn my head away from his all-seeing gaze, but he doesn't let me.

"I'm sorry. I..."

My words are cut off as he slams his mouth onto mine. I gasp in shock, but he takes that opportunity to lick inside my mouth, running his tongue along mine in a slow, sensual caress.

I am too stunned to move, too overwhelmed with lust to even try to get away, and I don't want to. I throw my arms around him, pulling him even closer. Someone moans loudly, but I have no idea if it was him or me. I don't care either. I spent the day thinking I ruined any chance with him. Now that he is here, I know I can't hold back.

He walks forward, forcing me to take steps back until he has me pressed against the wall, his body holding me there. He kicked my door closed as we passed it. I can feel his hardness, his need for me as he rubs against me. It is all so much, so thrilling.

He runs his hands down my sides, feeling every curve, every single part of me. His hands settle on my ass as he lifts me into his arms. I wrap my legs around him as he begins to grind against me. The feel of his jeans against my barely covered mound is just the perfect amount of pressure to send me reeling.

I pull my mouth away from his so that I can groan at the feel of him against me.

"Colby," I say because right now, that is apparently the only word I know.

"Fuck, Ember. This isn't why I came here. But I can't stop. Tell me to stop, honey," he says as he licks and nips his way down my neck. He is ravenous like he can't get enough of me, and I am right there with him.

"Don't ever stop," I manage to say between breaths.

My robe has slipped open, and he takes advantage by latching onto one of my breasts, licking and sucking feverously, switching back and forth, giving both nipples equal attention. He is growling like a wild animal, but that only feeds my need for him.

"You are so fucking beautiful, Em. So amazing," he groans as he slides me to the floor, dragging his lips along every inch of my skin.

I can't really feel the floor beneath my feet, can't focus on anything but the sensations flowing through my body. Each touch, each kiss makes me feel like I am flying, soaring through the air with nothing but freedom surrounding me.

I feel him tear open the rest of my robe, and glance down to see him on his knees in front of me. I am so lost in pleasure that I didn't even notice his movement. He places kisses on my stomach, then nips at my hip bones as his hands roam up and down my legs.

Just when I am about to push him where I need him the most, he stops and lays his forehead on my stomach. We are both panting heavily, sucking up all the oxygen in the room.

"Colby?" I ask, not sure what happened. Did he get a look at my arms and realize he doesn't want me? Did he see my hands and not want them to touch him?

I start to shrink back, trying to pull my robe back on, but he stops me.

"No, honey. Let me see you. All of you," he says, pulling my robe off me completely.

I haven't been naked in front of anyone in a long time, and definitely not since I became a mangled mess of what I used to be.

I close my eyes, afraid of his reaction once he really sees what I look like. A few tears slip free as I hold my breath, waiting for him to get up and walk away.

But then I feel his lips on my arms as he kisses up and down the raised, puckered skin. His tongue snakes out to lick along my wrist before he kisses all ten fingers. In between each kiss, he is whispering words.

"Beautiful."

"Gorgeous."

"Lovely."

"Stunning."

It's like he has a thesaurus in his pocket, listing every synonym for the word beautiful.

"You can't mean that," I whisper, afraid to say it too loud and make him realize what he is doing.

He stops his maddening torture to stand up. He leans in and kisses me before he pulls back and tears his shirt over his head.

The skin on his torso, along his chest and abdomen, is scarred, just like mine. You can tell where they performed skin grafts in an attempt to make him look normal. He has gone through just as much as I have. He is beautiful. The picture-perfect man in my eyes.

I reach forward but stop myself. I don't want to assume he wants my touch.

"Touch me, Em. Feel me. Feel how perfect we are for each other," he says as he takes my hands and places them on his skin.

He sucks in a breath as I run my hands on every inch of him. I drop to my knees and place kisses everywhere I can so that he can feel how much he is affecting me. I want him to feel the same acceptance he has shown me. I want him to understand that I am right here with him, at this moment that I never want to end.

I stop when I get to his pants, suddenly annoyed that they are in my way.

Without even thinking, I unbutton them and slide them down his legs, leaving him standing before me in just his boxer briefs. They are tented toward me and my mouth waters at the thought of seeing him, of tasting him, of running my tongue along every glorious inch of him. As I reach for them, ready to pull them off, I hesitate, worried that maybe I am taking this too far.

"Don't stop, Em. Please," he says. His voice is deep and full of need, and I love that I am making him feel as unhinged as I do right now.

I glance up at him and place one more kiss on his stomach before I pull his briefs off. His thick, pulsing shaft bobs out, pointing directly at me. I feel him lean forward, bracing his arms on the wall over my head. My back is still pressed to the wall, but I have plenty of room for what I want to do next.

I wrap my fingers around him, stroking him slowly. He lets out a hiss and closes his eyes, dropping his head back, telling me that he is enjoying my touch. When a small bead of precum leaks out, I lick it up before swallowing him down. His groans and moans of pure unadulterated pleasure encourage me as I lick and suck at him, running my tongue along the thick vein and around his head. He is so long and thick that I use my hand on the part I can't reach with my mouth. I work him fast and hard, wanting him to feel through my touch just how much him being here for me means in my heart.

"Enough," he says gruffly as he pulls me to my feet. "Bedroom?" His eyes are wild, his breaths coming in pants, and I smile, knowing I made him this way.

"Through there," I point as he hoists me up and over his shoulder.

I giggle for the first time in I have no idea how long and it causes him to stop.

"Was that a giggle, Em?" he asks as his hands roam up and down my thighs. He swats my behind, his hand lingering on my ass as he takes the final few steps into my room.

"Yes. It was a giggle," I say, just as shocked as he is at hearing it.

He tosses me onto my back on my bed and looms over me.

"I have a new favorite sound, and even if it kills me, I will hear it every day for the rest of our lives," he says right before he kisses me.

This kiss is so much more than any other. It is so deep and emotional. He moves slowly, rubbing himself against me. I feel his cock slip through my folds as he hits my clit with each thrust. I should be embarrassed by the sounds coming out of me, but I'm not, because it is him. It is Colby. A man who has taken a firm grasp of my heart in less than a day. I worry for just a moment that this is all moving too fast. That we should slow down and talk about everything, but the pressure in my core is about to explode, and any logical thoughts flitter away.

I spread my legs and his hips settle right there. His eyes stare deep into my soul and I can read the need in his face.

"I need to taste you," he says as he slides down my body, nipping and kissing a path down to my mound.

He shoulders himself into position, and I can feel his warm breaths on my clit.

"Please," I moan, not really sure what I am begging for. I know I would do anything he asked at this point.

"Do you need me, Em? Do you need me to make you scream my name with my tongue deep inside you?" he asks on a growl.

"Oh, God. Yes. Please. Do that!"

The first touch of his tongue is light, the barest of contact. I moan, loving it, but needing more. So much more.

"More. Please, Colby. More," I beg. He has me right where he wants me, and I wouldn't want to be anywhere else.

"Fuck, Em, you beg so nicely," he says right before he dives in and absolutely devours me.

His tongue works magic on me, running deep inside me and all around my folds until he settles on my clit, sucking hard. He is growling and groaning as he works, making sure that each swipe of his tongue hits me perfectly. My hands grip his hair as I thrust myself into his waiting mouth, grinding against him. When I cum, it is more powerful than anything I have ever experienced, and I scream his name, just as he said I would.

"**F**uck, Em. I never want to leave your pussy. I could spend the rest of my life making you come undone for me," I say as I prowl back up her body. Her taste is forever imprinted on my tongue.

I settle my dick at her entrance, leaning my weight on my elbows just beside her head. Her hair is spread around her, wild and disheveled, but she is still the most beautiful woman I have ever seen.

I stop, pausing for a moment to take it all in. This is the moment when she becomes mine. I don't want to scare her, but I need her to know what this means to me.

"Em. You need to tell me now if you aren't ready for this. Because once I am inside you, once I thrust my dick inside your tight, hot, wet pussy, you'll be mine. Forever. There will be no going back. We can go as slow as you want, but I don't move backward. If you don't want this, I'll wait. You are worth it. You are worth everything," I say as I stare deep into her eyes.

I watch her closely for any sign that this isn't what she wants. She runs her hands up my body and settles them on my cheeks.

"I want you, Colby. I want us. I didn't realize how empty I was until you found me. I need you, so badly," she says, pulling me down into a kiss so powerful I can feel it in my bones.

I don't wait any further as I slam my cock deep inside her. We both cry out from the intensity, from the overwhelming emotion behind this moment. She locks her ankles behind my back and pulls, forcing me to move inside her. I know at this moment; I have found my forever. It isn't just about the amazing way she is making me feel, it isn't about the sex. No. It is about the way my heart is about to beat out of my chest. It is so full of a powerful need to take care of this woman. To shelter her and love her with everything I am.

"You feel so amazing, so perfect, honey," I manage to say. I am clenching my teeth and my ass to keep myself from spilling inside her already. You'd think this was my first time. But she just feels that damn good.

"You feel like home, Colby."

I lose it at her words because that is exactly how I feel. I begin to slam into her with everything I have. She gives just as good as she takes as with each thrust, she raises her hips up to meet me. I reach down with one hand to rub her clit, wanting her to cum at least once more before we finish. Not that this will be the last time I take her tonight. No, I will never get enough of her.

"Harder! Please," she cries out, raking her fingernails down my back.

We are both sweating from the exertion, but that just means that I will get to clean her up in the shower later. Yeah, I can definitely picture taking her in the shower. Her bent over, ass in the air, as I pummel her from behind.

"Come for me, Em. Come so fucking hard," I say as I fight off my impending explosion. I know that when I cum, it is going to be the hardest I have ever cum in my life. The tingling at the base of my spine tells me as much. As much as I want that, I want to hold off. I want the anticipation of it, the build-up that will lead to the most amazing feeling in the world. Sometimes that is more intense than the act itself.

With one final pump, she cums, screaming my name, and I can't hold back any longer. I roar out my release, shooting my seed deep inside her.

"Fuck, Em!"

I collapse to the side of her, immediately pulling her into my arms. I don't want any space between us.

She sprawls across my chest, gasping for breath. Her fingers are running up and down my stomach, gently stroking the marred skin.

"You okay, babe?" I ask. "I swear this isn't why I came here. But when I saw you in your robe looking so goddamned beautiful, I didn't have a choice."

"You had no choice, huh?" she says as she pinches my nipple.

"Hey! Don't start something you can't finish soldier," I warn, which earns me another giggle. "God, I love that sound, Em."

She settles, laying her head back down on my chest and I hold her close, running my fingers along her back.

We are quiet for a while, each of us absorbing the intensity and implications of everything we just shared. We both said things that suggest a long future ahead of us, but as quiet as she is now, I worry that she is doubting everything.

Just as I am about to say something, she speaks. It is whispered, and so quiet I am not sure she meant for me to hear it.

"I'm sorry."

I push her onto her back so that I can look into her eyes. Panic starts to fill me as I think maybe she means she is sorry for what just happened.

"What are you apologizing for?" I ask. There are tears pooling in her eyes and I cup her face, leaning down to kiss her.

She pushes me back. "I'm sorry I ran from you. I'm sorry I am such a mess. I'm sorry I..."

I cut her off by slamming my mouth onto hers. I kiss her feverously, not willing to let her finish those words. She is apologizing for what she has been through? Fuck that.

The only thing able to stop me from taking her again is my incessant need to ease her pain.

"Honey, you have nothing to apologize for. Nothing at all. I understand, well, I don't know everything, but I get where you are coming from. I may not have been through the same thing as you, but I dealt with my own issues. Let me help you, Em. I want to be here for you. Don't push me away," I say.

A few of those tears fall and I kiss them away.

"I don't know how," she says, choking back a sob. "I'm so scared, Colby."

"Talk to me. Why are you afraid?" I ask. I know I shouldn't push her after everything she went through today, but she needs to understand that I am here, that I am with her no matter what.

I watch the emotions play across her face. I can tell she wants to talk to me; she wants to open up, but the fear wins out, at least right now. She breaks down, sobbing as she pulls me down on top of her. She cries for a while, so I pull her close. I roll onto my back and pull her on top of me. I hold her as she falls apart. Each tear, each sob tears me up inside. I want to take it all away. I want to comfort her; I just don't know how.

It takes a while for the tears to stop. Through it all, Colby just holds me, rubbing his hands all over my body. I appreciate that he doesn't say anything. I have come to hate the empty words people say like *it will be okay* and *just give it time.* My family says those things to me all the time and though I know they mean well, they just hurt to hear.

For a while there, I wasn't sure things were going to be okay. I wasn't sure I would make it. Through all the surgeries, the pain, the fear, I worried I was losing myself. I haven't felt normal, if that is even a thing anymore, since... well since I met Colby, today. Today was the first time in a long time that I felt like I could talk openly. That no matter what I said, I wouldn't be judged. I know that my family and the doctors, hell, even my squad, don't hold any ill will toward me for what happened. No. The blame comes only from inside.

There is a strong connection between the two of us, like an invisible pull. After I ran away from him today, there was more than embarrassment at my cowardice. It was pain – the kind you feel when you are away from someone important.

I know now what I need to do. I know it is going to hurt like hell, but he deserves the truth. If we are going to move forward, this has to happen. Now.

"Romeo and I were on assignment with my commanding officer, Zeb," I say. This will be the first time I have said any of this out loud in almost a year. I feel the air thicken around me like someone is trying to keep it from me, but I fight against it.

"Take your time, love," Colby says as his arms tighten around me.

Love.

Hearing him say that is the only force strong enough to keep me going right now. I know he will hear everything I have to say, no matter how terrible, how incredibly painful it is.

"We were supposed to clear the road so that the convoy could move through that night. I took Romeo ahead, allowing him to work. We had been together for eight years so we could read each other's emotions without any signs. He knew his job and I knew mine," I say. Now that I have started, I have this immense need to finish. The words are pouring out of me as the movie plays in my head.

"Romeo worked fast, but I could tell something was off. He wasn't giving me any signs that he found anything, but I knew something was putting him on edge. His ears were twitching all around, his head jerking from side to side as he worked. It was like he could sense something coming. Once he cleared that particular section, I told Zeb he needed a break. I set him up in the front seat of our Humvee with some water and a snack. I gave him one last kiss..." I have to stop for a moment. It feels like I am right back there with him. There are so many things I would have said to him had I known it was the last time I would get the chance.

"I'm right here, Em. You are right here with me," Colby says as he places my hand right over his heart. The strong beat of it on my palm centers me, bringing me back to the present.

I take a few deep breaths before I continue.

"I gave him a kiss and told him I would be right back. I closed the door and went around to the other side to talk to Zeb. I wanted to let him know that something had Romeo spooked. As we talked, Zeb led me away from the vehicle. We stopped about twenty feet from it. And that's when the missile hit."

I fight the urge to break down again. I breathe deeply, trying to focus on Colby's heady scent. He continues to run his fingers along my body, knowing I need the touch right now. After a few minutes, I finally calm down enough to finish.

"The vehicle was immediately engulfed in flames. Romeo was screaming, howling for me, but I couldn't get to him. Zeb was trying to hold me back. There was another team not too far from us, clearing a different area. When they saw the explosion, they came. I wouldn't stop trying to get to him. I couldn't. I fought free of their hold and ran right to the driver's side door. I yanked and pulled with everything I had, not caring about the pain racing up my arms. The initial hit bent the frame of the Humvee though and I couldn't get the door open. Colby, I swear I tried! I tried... so hard. But nothing worked! I watched the fire take him from me. I watched him burn, listened to him cry for me! I stared into his eyes. Eyes that were filled with confusion, with fear. He didn't understand. *I* didn't understand. How could this be happening? So many people were pulling on me, trying to tear me away from him. But I knew... I knew I had to stay there and be with him, even if I couldn't hold him and tell him everything would be alright. I had to let him see me. I kept screaming 'I'm sorry', but it was no use. When they finally pulled me back, it was just in time. The damn thing blew right in front of us. Sent us all flying. And that was it. He was gone. The next few months are a blur. Hospitals. Surgeries. Therapy. But none of it mattered. Because I failed him. *I failed him.* He knew it was coming. That's why he was so worked up. He knew they were there, but I didn't listen. I let him die, Colby!"

By the time the last words are out, Colby has completely wrapped himself around me, holding me as I finally say the words that have been bottled up inside. I may have told my story to Antonia, but not like that. Not raw, and unfiltered, and punishing like that. Part of me feels relieved that I finally said the words out loud.

Colby doesn't say anything. He just holds me. He does exactly what I need him to do by letting me completely fall apart in his arms. There are no empty promises, no false words of encouragement. He knows. He knows I just need him.

"There is not a second of a single day that goes by that I don't wish I could change that moment. I wish I would have kept him with me out of the Humvee. I wish I would have held him longer, told him I loved him, let him know just how much he meant to me. I even wish I would have died with him, so he wasn't alone. So, I didn't have to live with this gut-wrenching, all-consuming fear every day. Every. Single. Day, Colby. It should have been me," I say in an all-out sob.

"Don't say that Ember. Don't you dare even think that! I hate that you went through that. I hate every goddamned part of it. But don't ever say you want to die. I just found you. I will not lose you," Colby says, a few tears of his own falling.

"It hurts. So much. I don't know how to deal with this pain anymore. I don't want to get close to anyone because I don't want to feel this again. I am so terrified, Colby, all the time. I have pushed my family away because I don't want the pain of losing them. I ran from you because I don't want to lose you, too. I feel..." I have to stop because it is getting too deep, too heavy for me.

"Don't stop, Em. Say what you mean. Don't hold anything back," Colby says, urging me to continue.

"I feel, so fucking much for you already. I can't imagine what it would feel like if I lost you," I say.

I can feel the trembling in my body. I know that the panic is setting in. I fight against it, but it is too strong.

I don't know how he manages to do it, but Colby completely wraps his entire body around me. I feel totally cocooned in his arms. "Don't let it win, Em. Fight with me. Breathe deep, let it go. Let the pain go," he says as he gets me to mimic his breathing.

We lay together like that, taking deep full-lunged breaths for a long time. He doesn't let up, not even the slightest, the entire time.

I feel the tension leave my body all at once. It is as if my mind finally realizes it is safe.

As I drift off to sleep in Colby's arms, I realize this is what I have needed all this time. Not just someone to bare my soul to. Colby. I just needed Colby.

She fell asleep a while ago, but I won't let go. I can't. My hold on her is just as firm as it was hours ago when the panic tried to take her from me. I knew if I let her spiral too far, she would try to run. I know because I've been there. I know what it feels like to have your world come crashing down around you. I know the pain and agony of living when others didn't. Romeo may not have been human, but he was her partner. That doesn't make his death any less painful than any of my brothers that I lost.

I have been awake for hours just holding her. I can't find sleep, not after everything she told me. Knowing what she went through, hell, there's no wonder she built her walls up so high. I get her fear of losing people, but I hate that she has let that keep her from living. That is the first thing we will work on.

Together.

I'm never letting her go. I knew there was something there the first time I saw her. I could feel it. But after spending just one day with her, after getting to know the woman behind the walls, I know I love her. I love her so fucking much and I don't give one good goddamn if people say it is too fast. The heart knows. The one thing I learned in the Army, the one thing that was drilled into me so hard that I live by it every day, is to trust your gut.

Well, my gut says that this woman is my life now. I don't care if it takes me the rest of my life, I will chase her. I would follow her to hell and back just to be near her.

I feel her stirring a little bit, so I loosen my hold on her.

"No. Don't let me go," she says in a sleepy voice.

"Never, Em. I'm never letting you go," I say, placing a kiss on the top of her head.

She tilts her face up so that she can look at me. Her eyes are puffy and red from her crying, but she still takes my breath away.

"You're still here," she says. The relief in her voice is a punch to the gut. Did she really think I would leave?

"I hate to tell you this, honey, but you are stuck with me. Ain't no exterminator around that could get rid of my stubborn ass," I say.

She giggles and my entire world is complete.

"I'm sor..." she starts, but I put my fingers over her mouth.

"No. No, Em. No more apologizing. No more looking back, no more wishing things had gone differently, no more fear. I know it is going to take you a while to understand this, but I am never leaving you. Something happened when I first saw you. Something clicked, in here," I say, placing her hand right over my heart. "My entire world shifted, and everything fell into place."

"Colby," she says in a whisper.

"Oh, I'm not done, Em. In fact, I'm just getting started."

I lean down and kiss her, pouring everything I can into it. Her hands find their way into my hair as she tries to pull me closer. The words are right on the tip of my tongue. I want to tell her I love her so fucking much, but I also know I have already completely overwhelmed her with everything that has happened. I wasn't lying when I said this isn't what I came here to do. My plan, or lack thereof, was to come over and just talk, let her know that I am here for her. But seeing so much of her on display, her beauty, her scars, everything, was too much to handle.

Before I can take things further, my phone goes off.

"Shit," I say as I grab it to turn off my alarm.

"What's wrong?" she asks, and I hate that the vulnerability is back in her voice.

"Nothing. It's just my alarm. I have to be at work in a couple of hours," I say, leaning down to kiss her again.

"Where is Tonka?" she asks. I love that she is thinking about him.

"He's at home. Don't worry. I explained everything to him," I say as if that is the most normal thing in the world.

"You did, did you? And what did you tell him?" she asks with a smile.

"That I was leaving to get the woman of my dreams."

She tucks her chin to her chest as a rosy tinge takes her cheeks.

"Hey," I say, pulling her face up with my finger under her chin. I did a lot of thinking last night and I came up with a sort of game plan. But now that I am about to say it out loud, I am worried about how she will react.

I lean down and place a kiss on the tip of her nose.

"Hear me out, okay?" I say, the nerves filling me up, trying their hardest to overtake me.

She raises her hand and cups my cheek. "Why are you nervous?" she asks.

"Because I don't want to scare you. I had an idea last night while I was holding you in my arms," I start, pausing for a moment to catch my breath. *Why is this so damned hard?*

"Just say it, Colby, please. You're scaring me," she says. I watch as she starts to shrink in on herself.

"No, honey, no. Scared was the wrong word. Man, I am fucking this all up," I say as I run my hand through my hair.

"Do you... are you... wow, this sucks. Are you breaking up with me? Fuck, are we even together?" she says. I can see the panic rising in her.

"No. I mean, yes. I mean... wow, we are really, really bad at this, aren't we?" I say and we both let out little chuckles. I sit up so that my back is against the headboard and pull her up so that she is straddling me.

I take her face in my hands. "Look at me, Em. Yes, we are together. We are so much more than just together. And, no, I am not breaking up with you. I thought that maybe you would want to come to work with me today. I want to spend as much time as possible with you. I want to get to know you. I want to know everything about you, and I want to share everything with you. I know it will be hard, but I saw how you were with Tonka. I think this would really be good for you. You don't have to do anything but hang out."

I watch her eyes the entire time I am talking. I can see each emotion play out there. There's joy and what I hope is love, but more concerning is the fear and worry.

I cup her cheeks. "Baby, look at me. I am not forcing you to do anything. And honestly, this is more about spending time with you than anything else."

"Are you... trying to fix me?" she asks, and I want to punch myself in the face. Of course, that's how this sounds.

"No! No. I don't think you need fixed Em. You're not broken," I say quickly.

"But I am broken, Colby. Don't you see? There are times I don't even know who I am anymore," she says.

I pull her into my arms, holding her tight with her head against my chest. "Then we will figure it out. Together. You aren't alone in this anymore, Em. I am going to be by your side, holding your hand through everything. I just need you to take the first step. I won't force you to do anything, but I do need your help," I say.

She is quiet for a while. I didn't say anything I would take back – I meant every word. They are words that have been said to me, back when I was on the road to recovery. I am willing to do anything for her, to go above and beyond for her, but she has to be willing to try. And the thing is, I know she is, she just needs a little encouragement. And that is what I'm here for.

It is amazing how quickly someone can become your entire world. I was never one to look into the future, to make plans. I have always lived day by day because when you don't know if you will make it to the next day, you focus on the present.

That all changed yesterday when I saw Ember. I immediately saw my future, and it was her. I could see her walking down an aisle to me. I could see her pregnant with our children. I could see us old, and gray surrounded by a house full of dogs and children. I want that future. I want it so bad I can feel it in my bones.

I am so lost in my head that I almost don't hear her response.

It is just one word, but it is the most important word I have ever heard.

"Okay."

I can't sit still. My leg is bouncing up and down, my hands are shaking. I am chewing on the inside of my lips, worrying them back and forth. I have pretty much been freaking out since I agreed to go to work with Colby. He can see it; I know he can. He hasn't stopped touching me since I agreed. Even now that we are in his car on the way, his hand is resting firmly on my thigh, almost as if he is afraid I will open the door and barrel roll away from him. Don't tempt me, the thought had crossed my mind.

But he has done his best to distract me from the moment I agreed. Right after the word left my mouth, he had me out of bed and in the shower. He spent an exuberant amount of time making sure I was clean. I am not complaining about that at all. In fact, aside from last night, it was the most amazing moment of my life. The second the water turned on, he dropped to his knees in front of me and drove me to the brink of insanity with his talented tongue. I then returned the favor, because, well, I wanted to. I worshiped his amazing cock with my mouth, swallowing him down. The way he grasped my hair and thrust into me is permanently etched in my brain, and I know I will remember it for the rest of my life.

Then, he bent me over and took me from behind as the water rained down all around us. There was no hesitation, no build-up – just pure, raw, unadulterated pleasure. I completely lost myself in him. I could feel every emotion, could feel the love flowing between us.

I wanted to say those words, I wanted to tell him just how much I feel for him, but I am worried that I would only be opening myself up to more pain. This is so new, so fresh between the two of us. I have never fallen in love before, so I am not sure how it is supposed to work. I am pretty sure that it is not supposed to happen overnight. But maybe that's it. Maybe I am so broken that I can't even fall in love the right way. He would probably think I am crazy.

"Hey," he says, squeezing my leg to get my attention. He releases my leg only to take my hand and brings it up to his lips where he places gentle kisses on my knuckles. The action stops me from shredding the edge of my shorts, at least that side. "I am proud of you, Em."

I turn to look at him. "Why? I am a complete mess over here. I don't even know if I will have the strength to get out of your car, let alone go inside the building."

"We'll take it step by step. There is no pressure at all, Em," he says as he pulls into an apartment complex.

"I thought we were going to your office," I say, confused for a moment.

"We are. I just have to run in and grab Tonka first. Can't leave him behind. If he finds out I went to work without him, I will never hear the end of it."

I laugh at that, just picturing him having it out with Tonka has me smiling.

"There it is. You are so beautiful, Em," he says as he leans over and places a kiss on my forehead. "Wait here. I'll be right back."

"You don't want me to see your place?" I ask, not sure why I can't just come with him. I don't like the thought of being away from him right now.

He pauses, looking up and down my body. "I do, and I will show it to you. But if you come in right now, we won't be leaving for a very long time, and I have some classes to teach today."

My face heats up at the thought and he growls.

"Don't. Don't even tempt me right now, Em. I am hanging on by a thread and it is more than ready to snap. Plus, I don't really want to traumatize Tonka with all the things I want to do to you. Not yet at least," he says as he kisses me quickly and then climbs out of the car.

I watch him jog up the flight of stairs to his second-floor apartment, appreciating the view the entire time. He really is the most attractive man I have ever seen. He obviously still keeps in shape. He isn't overly muscular but has enough definition to make me drool just thinking about his body. Believe me, I spent a good amount of time last night and this morning becoming very well acquainted with him.

The door opening makes me jump and I feel Tonka climb into the car behind me. He practically dives over the seat and into my lap, reining kisses all over me.

"Tonka!" Colby yells, and Tonka immediately sits, right on my lap.

Without even thinking, I throw my arms around Tonka, pulling him in for a hug.

"It's okay, Colby. Really, it is," I say, rubbing Tonka's ears with both of my hands.

I'm not sure why, but suddenly, the sight of my mangled hands rubbing Tonka's fur makes me jerk back like I touched something I shouldn't have. My face pales and I start to sweat.

Tonka senses my discomfort and climbs into the back, sitting calmly as I lose my mind.

Colby gets in on his side and immediately takes my face in his hands.

"Hey. Hey. Look at me, Em. Look in my eyes," he says calmly.

I can't force myself to move my hands. I am holding them up in front of me, staring at them like I am seeing them for the first time. And, in a way, it's because I am. I can't remember the last time I left the house without my gloves on. I normally go out of my way to keep my hands hidden, even when they are gloved because even the gloves draw attention. But from the moment we left my place this morning, and even before that, I didn't stop once to think about it. I didn't worry myself about going outside. I didn't focus on what I would wear and what people would think. I didn't think about anything but being with Colby and taking this next big step.

"Colby," I say in a whisper, a tear running down my cheek.

"I'm so sorry, Em. I shouldn't have suggested this. It's not a problem. I'll take you back home, and," he says, rambling so fast his words are jumbled together.

"No. Colby, look," I say, holding my hands up for him to see. I can tell he doesn't understand where I am going with this.

He takes both of my hands in his and holds them against his chest. "What is it, honey? What's wrong?"

I sniffle, fighting back more tears. "I forgot my gloves. I didn't even think about wearing them this morning. This... is the first time I have left the house without them in a year." My voice is quiet yet filled with wonder.

I can see when Colby finally gets it because his face erupts in a glorious smile. He brings both of my hands up to his mouth where he presses his lips to them, holding them there as he smiles. I watch as he places gentle kisses along the scars. The raised skin is still so sensitive, and the slight pressure and wetness from his lips feel like freedom.

"You are so amazing, Em."

"No, Colby. It's you. You did this. You had me so focused on taking the next step that I didn't worry about it. Thank you. Thank you for helping me," I say as I lean forward and kiss him. I know there is still a long road ahead of me, and that my recovery is nowhere close to complete. But this feels like a huge step forward, and I suddenly feel full of hope.

Tonka takes the opportunity to dive on top of us, smothering us both in wild, crazy kisses.

"Ugh, Tonka. I don't need your tongue in my mouth, man," Colby says, pushing him to the back.

I giggle as Tonka decided to take the chance at shoving his tongue in my mouth.

Colby shoves him to the back and starts the car. He reaches for my hand, and I don't hesitate to wrap my fingers in his.

"Are you ready, Em?" he asks, his eyebrows raised.

I nod. "As long as I have you I am."

He leans over and presses his lips to mine. I want to take it further, but he quickly pulls back, giving me that warning glare again.

"Hanging on by a thread, Em," he says as he puts the car in drive.

Power rushes through me at being able to unhinge such a strong, amazing man. I sit forward as he pulls out onto the road. I am still nervous and jumpy at the thought of what I am about to do but knowing that Colby is with me gives me just enough strength to try.

Ember is shaking again. I can feel her body trembling as I pull into the parking lot at my office. I invited her today because I have a couple of classes with some new puppies, just starting the training process. The families that are working with them are great and I think that it is the perfect way to ease her into this process.

Dave will be here, too, and I know that meeting him will help as well. Dave and I were injured at the same time, and while my scars are hidden under my clothes, he wears his with honor. Both of his legs are a mess from the burns, but he doesn't hide them. He went through a lot but is just so happy that he survived. He actually does some motivational speaking, sharing our story and his recovery. He is a true hero with everything he does for our fellow brothers and sisters.

I pull into my spot and park the car. Tonka is bouncing around in the back seat, anxious to go inside. He loves it here. He gets a lot of attention from everyone, plus he gets to show off his skills as I use him as an example in training.

I go around and let him out the back. He sprints to the front door of the building and waits.

When I open Ember's door, she doesn't move. I can see her legs shaking and she is shrinking back in on herself. Her hands are pulled inside her long sleeves and her chin is tucked firmly to her chest.

I squat down next to her, reaching out to cup her face. "Em, if this is as far as you can go today, that's perfectly fine. I am already so proud of how far you have come. I can take you back home now."

I know she wants to do this. She is so strong and brave, and I can already see her sense of determination to do this. I watch as the emotions play across her face. The fear is fighting against everything as she battles with the demons of her past. Unless you have been through something like this, you wouldn't understand the emotional turmoil that can happen inside your mind. It is a war with every single part of you. Each aspect of your personality fights for control against the memories that will never go away. We carry them with us wherever we go, it just becomes about being able to manage them. There is no control over them, just learning to deal with the damage they cause inside you.

She closes her eyes for a moment, and I watch what parts of the battle I can see. These are the parts I wish I could fight for her, but unfortunately, I can't. That is the worst part of the road to recovery, there is only so much you can do for someone. A lot of it is internal and they have to do it for themselves.

Eventually, she takes a deep breath and opens her eyes. There is a look of fierce determination as she nods once and turns to face me.

"You won't leave me, right?" she asks.

"Never," I say adamantly as I pull her out into my arms.

She rests her head on my chest and wraps her arms around my waist. I run my hands up and down her back, through her hair, and down her arms until I have them grasped in front of us.

A throat clears behind us, and I turn to see Dave standing there with a look of amusement.

"Well, who is this gorgeous specimen?" he asks.

I turn to face him, pulling Ember to my side as I wrap my arm around her.

"Hey, Dave. This is my Ember. Em, this is my partner in crime, Dave," I say with pride.

Ember has her arms wrapped around herself as she tries to hide her hands. Thankfully, though, Dave is not one to shy away from anyone. He reaches out and pulls her hand out, bringing it to his mouth and placing a kiss there.

When he pulls it back, he stares at it in wonder.

I can see Ember trying to pull her hand back, but he doesn't let her.

"What the fuck?" he says. "How in the hell can you make burns look so goddamn sexy, Ember? That's just not fair."

He takes a step back and puts one leg out in front of him, turning it back and forth so she can see his scars. "Mine look like someone took a fucking cheese grater to my skin. Damn, woman, you are beautiful!"

I watch Ember blush and I pull her closer. "Alright, asshole. That's enough ogling my woman."

"It's nice to meet you," Ember finally says.

"Come on, you two. I want to get everything set up before the first group gets here," Dave says as he turns to head inside.

"Ready?" I ask Ember.

She nods. "I think I am."

She takes a deep breath and then follows behind Dave. Tonka runs up to her like this is the best day of his life and I laugh.

• • • •

Dave and I walk Ember through what to expect with the first class. This will be the third time this group has come in, and all the puppies are less than six months old. It is a big process, getting these dogs ready for service, and we depend heavily on the families to help. Ember takes it all in stride until the first family arrives.

She slinks off to the side, taking a seat in the back of the room. I don't say anything because I know this is going to be hard for her. I want her to progress at her own pace. I figured it would take her a few weeks to work up to participating in one of the classes.

We are getting everyone set up when the last family arrives. The puppy, a German Sheppard, comes racing into the room, ready to play with his friends. I glance over to Ember and see her face lose all color. She looks like she is ready to throw up.

I can see from here that she is gasping for breath, clutching at her chest before she gets up and runs out the door.

I turn to Dave, and he simply juts his chin in her direction, giving me the okay to go after her.

"I'll be right back," I say as I take off.

I find her at the end of the parking lot on the same bench where we met. She is in the same position, leaning forward with her elbows on her knees and her head in her hands as she succumbs to the panic. My heart is breaking for her as I watch her fall apart again.

"Baby," I say as I sit down next to her and fold her into my arms.

She comes easily, snuggling as close as possible.

"I can't, Colby. I tried, but I can't," she says between sobs.

"What happened? Can you tell me?" I ask.

"The sheppard," she says, sniffling.

It takes me a second to put it together. "Romeo was a German Sheppard?"

She nods but then presses her face into my chest.

"Oh, honey. I'm so sorry. I didn't know, or I wouldn't have suggested it," I say, feeling like a complete and utter ass for this.

"You didn't know," she says as she squeezes me tighter.

I pull her into my lap and rock her back and forth, doing everything I can to calm her. I hate that I can't make this all better. I feel so helpless, so completely useless.

This woman in my arms has been through so much, and it almost seems like every time we take a step forward, she gets knocked two steps back. She is trying, so hard. She is a fighter to her core. I know that she will eventually beat this entire thing, she will find her way through the fog so that she can be happy again. I just wish like hell that there was something I could do to take it all away, to fix it so that she didn't have to go through any of this pain.

She is finally calming down a little. Her breaths are coming more slowly, the tension fading from her body bit by bit. Just when I think the worst is over, the worst thing imaginable happens. The fire alarm in the building goes off and its loud, obnoxious screeching fills the air. Ember jumps so high she almost falls off my lap. I hold her closely, not sure how she is going to react.

I am stuck somewhere between worrying about Ember and worrying about what the hell is happening in my office. I don't know what the right thing to do is – stay and comfort Ember or go help inside. There are four families and several animals inside that could need me.

I am spared from my turmoil when Ember leaps off my lap and takes off at a sprint toward the front of the building. I leap to my feet and run after her, catching up just as the pulls the door open.

The sound cuts off as we get inside, and I see Dave standing next to one of the families. The young boy with them, Timmy if I remember right, is crying.

We head over to them as Timmy dives at my legs.

"I'm sorry, Mr. Colby. I didn't mean to pull the alarm. It was an accident," he says in between tears.

I squat down next to him and put my hand on his shoulder. "It's okay, Timmy. But we have to be more careful, okay."

He nods and turns into his mother's open arms. "I'm sorry, Colby. I only turned my back for a second," she says, but I hold my hand up to stop her.

"No worries. Accidents happen," I say.

Everyone heads back to the center of the training floor, but I turn to Ember. She has a look of shock on her face as she watches everyone go.

"Em? Talk to me, honey," I say as I place my hands on her shoulders and turn her to face me.

"I didn't even think, Colby. The dogs, the kids. I knew I had to help," she says as if she did something wrong.

"Hey," I say, placing my hands on her neck and tilting her head up with my thumbs so that she has to look into my eyes. "Do you realize what you just did?"

She shakes her head back and forth slowly, still fighting the shock.

"Em, you ran right into the building at the sound of the alarm. You had no idea what you were running into, but you did it anyway. Your first thought was to help," I say, hoping that she sees the monumental breakthrough she just had.

Her eyes widen and her mouth falls open.

Tonka picks that moment to come up to us. He drops his stuffed kitty at her feet and sits down right in front of her. The way he is staring up at her in wonder makes it seem like he understands exactly what happened. I swear animals know so much more than we give them credit for.

He nudges Ember's hand, and she glances down at him. He lets out a short bark.

She squats down in front of him and places both hands on his ears, rubbing him just the way he likes. "Are you okay, Tonka?"

He inches closer to her until he is almost on top of her. In a move that completely shocks me, he leans forward and rests his forehead on hers. Ember doesn't need any further encouragement as she leans forward and closes her eyes as she leans into him.

If I wasn't already completely in love with her, I am now. The two beings in front of me have my whole heart, and the fact that they are bonding like this after something that should have been traumatic to both fills me with so much love that I can't contain it any longer.

"I love you," I just about shout out, causing both Ember and Tonka to stare at me.

"Wh... what did you say?" Ember asks hesitantly.

I clear my throat so I can do this right. I lean down and take her hands, pulling her to her feet so that I can look her in the eyes.

I cup her cheeks and stare deep into her eyes. "I said, I love you. I know we just met yesterday, but if I learned anything in the service, it's to trust my gut. And my gut, and everything else in me is telling me that you are the one, Ember. I love you, so fucking much. I don't expect you to say it back, not yet anyway. I just need you to know that I am in this with you. I will fight beside you. Not that you need me. You are so absolutely amazing on your own."

She stares at me with her mouth hanging open and I worry that I freaked her out.

"Dammit. I'm sorry. I shouldn't have said anything. Just... forget I said anything, okay," I say. I turn to head into my office, my tail tucked firmly between my legs. I don't make it two steps before I feel the all too familiar grip of her rough hand on mine.

I don't turn around because I am terrified of what I might find. Did I just fuck this up? Did I just blow the best thing that has ever happened to me?

"I love you, too, Colby. So much. I was scared to say anything. I'm still scared," she says so quietly.

I turn around, not able to help it anymore, and pull her to me, probably too roughly, but I can't control myself right now. She loves me!

"I'm scared too, Em. But I know this is right. I can feel it with everything in me," I say.

"I can't lose you, Colby. I wouldn't survive it," she says, tears falling down her face.

"I'm right there with you. But we can't let our fears keep us from living. I want to give this a chance, Em. I *know* we will be amazing together. And, well," I say, leaning in to whisper in her ear. "The sex is fucking phenomenal."

She giggles and pulls back to look at me. She shrugs. "Eh. It was okay, I guess."

"Okay? I'll show you okay," I say, throwing her over my shoulder and stomping to my office. "We'll be back in a few minutes, Dave. Don't wait," I call over my shoulder before I close the door.

"There are families here, man," Dave calls back, and Ember just keeps on giggling as I slam the door and lock it.

Ember

Epilogue

The past few months have been the best, and worst, of my life. I know that sounds crazy, but with everything going on, it is the truth. Colby made it about a week after our declarations of love before he showed up at my apartment one night with Dave and a ton of boxes. They had me packed up and moved in with him in a few hours.

He started coming with me to my therapy sessions with Antonia. There were many sessions that I spent in tears as I talked about everything from that fateful day when my life changed forever. Colby would just sit quietly, holding my hand, as Antonia tried to help me through my emotions. I had never told her everything, just the bare minimum, skipping over the gory details of what happened. I hadn't been ready to tell my story, but with Colby's help, I have been slowly working through it.

I have been going to work with him every day. I have worked up to helping out occasionally in the classes. It is still difficult for me, but with Dave and Colby there, I am able to pitch in here and there. Colby wants me to do more, but he doesn't push, knowing that I need to do this in my own time.

Tonka and I have become best friends. To Colby's dismay, he tends to stick closer to me than him. He sleeps on my side of the bed and goes everywhere with me. Colby may pout about it, but I think he secretly loves our relationship because it means I am opening my heart even more.

Colby and Dave just finished the last class of the day, and we are cleaning everything up.

"I'll be right back," Colby says as he disappears into his office.

"You are doing really great, Ember," Dave says. "I'm so proud of how far you've come."

I glance down at my hands and smile. I haven't worn my gloves since the day after I met Colby. I can't bring myself to wear short sleeves yet, but I will get there eventually.

"Thanks, Dave. You and Colby have been so supportive. You've gone above and beyond what anyone else has ever done for me," I say.

He smiles, and is that a blush?

"Well, I just wanted you to know how thankful I am that you are in our lives. Take care of him, okay?" he says, jutting his chin behind me toward Colby's office.

"Of course," I say, confused as to what brought that up.

I am about to ask him when Colby comes back carrying a large box with a giant bow on it.

"What is that?" I ask. I notice Dave slip away as Colby places the box at my feet.

"Just a little present for my love," he says, leaning in to kiss me.

I narrow my eyes at him, suspicious of the way he is fidgeting, rocking back and forth on his feet.

"What's going on with you? Why are you nervous?" I ask.

He reaches up to wipe some sweat off his forehead.

"Nothing. I'm not nervous. Just... open the box, Em."

I tilt my head to the side, pursing my lips. He's up to something.

I squat down and pull the ribbon, releasing the lid of the box. I pull it off slowly, slightly scared of what might be inside.

Tears immediately pool in my eyes as I see the small bundle of fur curled up in a ball in one corner of the box. Its golden fur is fuzzy and sticking up in all directions, the way only a puppy's could.

"Colby," I manage to say as a few of the tears fall.

He steps over and scoops the little furball into his arms, holding it up so I can see it more clearly.

"I know we talked about this, and you said you weren't sure if you were ready, but I think you are. I think this is the next step we need to take together. Not only for you but for us," he says in a rush.

I tentatively reach out and stroke my finger along its nose. Its little eyes blink open sleepily and it yawns, letting out the most adorable little squeak. I cover my mouth with my free hand to keep the sob from slipping out as I continue to stroke it with my other hand.

Colby holds it out for me to take and I can't move. I am frozen by fear, but also love. Colby is always going out of his way to do things for me that he thinks will help me. From coming to therapy with me to allowing me to participate in classes at my own pace, he is always showing me his support and love. This is just another thing to add to the list of the amazing things he has done.

I reach out slowly and scoop the puppy into my arms. It is wearing a little bow, and something pokes my arm as I pull it close.

The puppy jumps to life and covers my face in kisses, licking every free space of skin it can reach. I am both laughing and crying, and my mind is racing. My emotions are all over the place. I slowly slide to the ground, my legs suddenly feeling like jelly and unable to hold my body up. The puppy continues to wiggle around in my arms, trying to get closer to me as I lay it on my lap.

Colby comes and kneels in front of me, wiping my tears away with his thumbs.

"I know I am springing this on you, but I also know you are ready for this," he says as he reaches down and unties the ribbon around the puppy's neck. When he pulls it out from around its neck, I gasp, unable to breathe.

"Colby?" I ask, not sure what else to say right now. It's like all the other words in the English language have been erased from my brain. My heart feels like a ticking time bomb, pounding against my chest.

Colby works at something on the ribbon, and when he raises his hands, there is a shiny diamond in between his fingers. The look on his face is one I will never forget. There is so much love shining in his gaze.

"These past few months have been the best of my life. I never... I mean, when I met you, no... sorry, I just... fuck. I'm screwing this all up," he says, completely flustered.

I reach out and touch him, running my fingers along his arm. He watches my fingers move, and his eyes find mine. He smiles as he takes my hand and raises it to his lips. After a deep breath, he winks at me and then continues.

"I had so many things I wanted to say to you, but now that you are sitting here in front of me, looking so damn beautiful and distracting, I lost them. But it doesn't matter. The only thing that matters is how much I love you. I don't want to wait, a single second longer, to marry you. I want my ring on your finger so that the entire world knows you're mine. So, please, put me out of my misery and end this embarrassing debacle of a proposal, and say you'll marry me."

I take the puppy from him and place it on the ground next to us so that I can crawl into his lap. I cup both sides of his face, leaning my forehead against his. I love this moment so much that I don't want it to end. I want to savor it, absorb it, so I never forget this feeling of complete and utter perfection.

I close my eyes and breathe in his heady, woodsy scent. My fingers are running back and forth along his stubble-covered jaw, making that wonderful scratching sound.

He clears his throat, breaking me out of my reverie. "Uh, Em? Can you please just answer? Either way. I'm about to keel over here from the anticipation."

I chuckle as the tears flow freely. "Yes."

"Yes? Yes, you'll marry me? Or, yes, you'll give me an answer? Oh, fuck it. I'm taking it as a yes, you'll marry me," he says, climbing to his feet with me in his arms. He slams his lips on mine, taking me in a kiss filled with so much intensity. He swings me around in the air, both of us laughing and crying.

The puppy starts whining as he finally puts me down. He doesn't go far, just steps back far enough to scoop the puppy in his arms.

"So, I was thinking we could call her Juliette," he says. "You know, in honor of Romeo."

"I love that, and I love you. Thank you, Colby. Thank you for... well, for everything. I know I wouldn't be here today if it weren't for you. You are... you're just... wow, we really do suck at this," I say, and we both laugh.

I hear the door to Colby's office open and turn to see Dave poking his head out. "Can we come out yet? We are dying in here," he says. I can tell he is holding Tonka back because he is jerking around and the door keeps slamming into the back of his head, causing him to wince and groan.

"Come out, you idiot. Come and congratulate us!" Colby says.

"About fucking time," Dave mumbles as he pushes the door open and Tonka comes rocketing out. Colby turns and holds his arms out as Tonka jumps into them, covering him in kisses.

I almost melt into a puddle on the floor when I hear what Colby says to him. "I did it, bud. I asked her. She's going to be my wife. And you'll be my best man, uh, dog."

I scoop Juliette into my arms, and the four of us come together in the messiest, kiss-filled, sloppiest hug ever. But it is better than anything I have ever been a part of. This is my family, my future, my forever. Right here, at this moment, I found everything, and I can't wait for the rest of our lives.

Colby
Bonus Epilogue

W hy the fuck is this so nerve-wracking? It's not like she isn't going to show up, right? It's our wedding, the moment we have both been waiting for.

Dave slaps me on the back, breaking me out of my temporary hell.

"What's got you so jittery?" he asks.

"I'm nervous as hell, man."

"Why? She isn't. She's as cool as a cucumber," he says.

"You saw her?" I ask incredulously.

"I just came from her room. You are going to absolutely die when you see her," he says.

"Oh, God. Is she okay?"

He laughs. "Will you please relax? She's perfect. She is stunning. And, for some unknown reason, she is excited to marry your sorry ass. I keep trying to talk her out of it, but it's no use."

"Fucker," I growl. I sober for a moment. "She's really okay?"

I am worried because just last week she was complaining about her dress. I have no idea what it looks like, but she said the sleeves were really uncomfortable and she kept spazzing over having to spend the day dealing with them.

Tears pool in Dave's eyes and I take a step back.

"What, man? You're freaking me out," I say.

"Just... wait until you see her," he says, clearing his throat.

My dad pokes his head into the room and tells us it's time. My heart is fluttering out of control, but I force my feet to move. Dave steps in and pulls me into a hug.

"Come on, Colby. Let's go get you married," he says.

I nod, just once, as he leads me out.

We are getting married in a field at the park. They set up tents for both Ember and me to get ready. As I take my spot in the front, I turn and take in all the happy faces. So many people are here to support us. Antonia is in the front, wiping her eyes as she smiles at me. My parents are sitting with Ember's mom – they both refused to have sides as we are now one big family. Everyone has truly gotten along so well, and they all pitched in to help us plan the wedding of our dreams.

I hear some music start somewhere. The tent at the back of the aisle opens, and Tonka and Juliette come trotting out. We got Tonka a fancy bowtie to wear, and Juliette is wearing a white tutu of sorts. Tonka is carrying the pillow with the rings, and Juliette has a basket of flowers in her mouth. There is a chorus of oohs and ahhs as they make their way to me. Both Ember and I insisted that the dogs be a part of our day.

When they make it to me, Dave slips their leashes on and tries to lead them over to the side. Tonka isn't satisfied with that as he slips his leash and comes over to sit by my side, looking up at me with his tongue hanging out.

I lean down and pet him. "It's okay," I tell Dave. "This is where he belongs."

Of course, Juliette is not happy about being left out, so she pulls Dave over so that she can sit on my other side. Everyone laughs, but it is perfect.

"Well. I guess that is settled," Dave says.

The music changes and everyone stands, ready to watch my beautiful bride enter.

I see Ember's dad first and watch as he holds his hand out.

My heart stops as I see a bare hand reach out and take his. Ember comes into view, and everything disappears. There she is, and she is perfect. Suddenly, everything calms inside me.

I gasp as I realize that there are no sleeves on her gown. She is wearing a strapless gown and her arms are completely bare. I can see the worry on her face as she looks around at everyone. I can't believe she put herself out there like this. I am constantly amazed at her, and this moment is no different.

Her eyes scan the crowd, and I watch as the panic starts to kick in. I am just about to go to her when her gaze locks on mine. My right-hand covers my heart at her sheer beauty.

I mouth the word *gorgeous* to her, and she smiles.

Her dad pats her hand, I guess to remind her that this is just getting started, and they start their walk toward me. It is only about thirty feet, but it feels like it takes them a year to make it to me. I am so anxious to have her next to me that I start toward them when they are only about halfway. The crowd laughs as I just about yank her away from her dad.

He just smiles and shakes his head at me, handing her over. Before I take her hand, I hold mine out to her father.

He takes my hand and leans into me. "Thank you. Thank you for giving me back my little girl."

I know what he means because he and I had this conversation when I went to him to ask for her hand. I had met her parents a few times over the course of our whirlwind romance. They were beyond thrilled that Ember was getting better. When I asked him if I could marry her, he said yes, if I promised him one thing.

"Anything," I said without hesitation.

"Don't let her lose her light again. You brought her back to us. And I can never repay you for that," he said, pulling me into a hug.

I nod at him now, letting him know that I understand. I would die before I let anything happen to her, and I told him as much. She is my entire world, and I will be damned sure that she knows it every day.

I watch him walk over to his wife as he wipes the tears from his eyes. When I turn back to Ember, I am almost knocked on my ass at her beauty.

I shake my head and step into her. "I can't wait," I say as I take her face in my hands and place my lips on hers. It is short, and not anywhere near what I wanted it to be, but we do have an audience, so I keep myself in check. At least for now.

When I pull back, there are a few chuckles around us.

"We aren't to that part yet, Colby," she whispers with a little laugh.

"I know, but I had no choice," I say with a shrug as I take her hand and lead her to the front.

The ceremony is short. We recite our vows and say the traditional words necessary.

The officiant barely has the words out when I grab Ember and tip her backward, slamming my mouth on hers. Everything fades away as I kiss my wife with everything that I am. It is deep and meaningful and so full of love.

Just like every time we touch, I lose all sense of reality. I feel a tap on my shoulder and growl as I turn to see Dave staring at me.

"What?" I growl.

"Uh, dude? You might want to save some of that for later," he says.

I stand up and scoop Ember into my arms. There are cat calls and hoots and hollers as I practically run down the aisle with her and straight into the tent at the back. Thankfully, someone closes the flaps behind me because I can't wait a second longer for this.

"Colby! What are you doing?" Ember asks as I start to unbuckle my pants.

"I need to be inside you, right this fucking second, Em. I cannot wait any longer," I say as I drop my pants and scoop her back into my arms.

I fumble with her dress, trying to find my way to heaven, but stop short and look at her with raised eyebrows.

"No panties, Em? You naughty girl," I say as I slide into her in one hard thrust.

I take her hard and fast because there is no way I can last. I am too worked up from the nerves and how gorgeous she is.

Once I finish, she looks at me and giggles. "Better?"

"Never, but that should hold me for at least a little bit," I say as I kiss her.

I place her on her feet and help her fix her dress before tucking myself back into my pants and zipping up.

Once we are both situated, I take her hands and bring them up to my mouth.

"There are no words big enough to describe how I feel right now. I wish there were because you deserve to know just how utterly, breathtakingly beautiful you look. I am beyond proud of you," I say, running my fingers up her arms.

"I wanted you to know how much I love you, Colby. When I was putting on my dress, I looked at the sleeves and realized I didn't need them. You are always telling me that I should own my scars. That I am beautiful inside and out. I wanted to show you I could do this," she says.

A tear slips from my eyes at her words. She did this for me.

"I can't wait to spend the rest of my life with you, Mrs. Masterson."

"Well, then Mr. Masterson. Let's get this party started," she says as she lifts the front of her dress up slightly and steps toward the front of the tent.

"I'm right behind you, wife," I say.

She pauses before she steps through.

"You with me?" she asks.

"Always."

Don't miss out!

Visit the website below and you can sign up to receive emails whenever Michelle Rider publishes a new book. There's no charge and no obligation.

https://books2read.com/r/B-A-FDQW-JTKGC

BOOKS 2 READ

Connecting independent readers to independent writers.

Did you love *Above and Beyond: Heart of a Wounded Hero*? Then you should read *When Eyes Meet*[1] by Michelle Rider!

[2]

If you looked up introvert in the dictionary, you would see a picture of Ali Ewing. After a traumatic event in high school, she isolated herself from everyone, convinced that if you don't let people in, they can't hurt you. Unfortunately, life doesn't always go as planned. As an aspiring mystery writer, she is forced to work with a partner for the final project in her creative writing class.

Of course, she is paired with Cole Buchanan, the guy she has crushed on since starting college. But the absolute kicker... the genre they are given for their scene is romance.

Cole has been very aware of Ali since he first laid eyes on her freshman year. He was beyond excited to finally have a class with her, and

1. https://books2read.com/u/mezerY

2. https://books2read.com/u/mezerY

even more ecstatic that they were paired together for the final project. As a sci-fi writer, he knows nothing of romance but is willing to give it a shot with Ali. The only problem is he can tell how nervous she is around him. He wants nothing more than for her to give him a chance, but when he finds out what happened to her in high school, he worries she will never trust him.

When Cole finally convinces Ali of his feelings, her past catches up to them and sends her running. Cole must fight hard to convince Ali of his love, but more importantly, that she can trust him. Everything depends on it, and he won't give up until he gets her back.

When Eyes Meet is a fast-paced story about learning to let go of the past so that you can find your future.

Read more at https://www.authormichellerider.com/.

Also by Michelle Rider

When Eyes Meet
Above and Beyond: Heart of a Wounded Hero

Watch for more at https://www.authormichellerider.com/.

About the Author

Michelle Rider writes short, sweet, and spicy romance books. Come for the heat but stay for the love. Connect with me on Instagram and Twitter (authormrider) or Facebook (Michelle Rider). Email me at authormichellerider@gmail.com. www.michelleriderauthor.com

If you love romantic suspense or contemporary romance, check out my books under Wendy Zuccarello. www.wendyzuccauthor.com.

Read more at https://www.authormichellerider.com/.